George's Family Tree
Rowan
Elise
George
Clover
Daisy
Bryony
Campanula
Cowslip

To
Child's World
Nursery
on Kristin
Distefano's
3rd
Birthday

For all the great-grandchildren
of Elsie Wetherall Hart (1888-1984)
who bought the Dolls' House
for her daughter in the 1920's,
who then gave it to the author
when she was a little girl,
and then George and Matilda moved in.

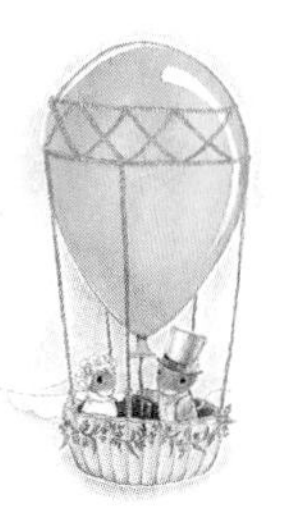

SIMON AND SCHUSTER BOOKS FOR YOUNG READERS
Simon & Schuster Building, Rockefeller Center, 1230 Avenue of the Americas New York, New York 10020

Library of Congress Cataloging-in-Publication Data
Buchanan, Heather S. George and Matilda Mouse and the dolls' house.
SUMMARY: George and Matilda Mouse get married and find the perfect home in an abandoned dolls' house.
[1. Mice–Fiction. 2. Dwellings–Fiction] I. Title. PZ7.B87713Gb 1988 [E] 88-4637
ISBN 0-671-66844-7
Manufactured in Italy 10 9 8 7 6 5 4 3 2 1

Published by the Simon & Schuster Juvenile Division.
Originally published in Great Britain by Methuen Children's Books Ltd., 1988.

GEORGE AND MATILDA MOUSE
and the DOLLS' HOUSE

Simon and Schuster Books for Young Readers
Published by Simon & Schuster Inc.

It was a very special day. This was the day George and Matilda Mouse were to be married at Tree Stump House. George's mother was icing the wedding cake and his sister Bryony was making trifle and arranging the food on the table. Clover and Cowslip were weaving a reed basket for the inflatable balloon that George was soon going to use to fetch Matilda. Everyone rushed around excitedly – especially George.

George had found the balloon caught high in a tree several weeks before and had climbed up to rescue it, carefully letting the air out so that it did not burst. Now all the mice puffed into it and it began to billow out into a lovely round shape. They tied its mouth securely to keep all the air in and decorated the reed basket with forget-me-nots.

When the wind direction was just right, the balloon lifted up into the air and George took off, floating away on the breeze.

Matilda had been up since dawn, brushing her whiskers and dabbing behind her ears with rose water. Oliver and Humphrey, her twin younger brothers, had been up early too, and had found her some rockroses to use as a headdress. She saved two to put behind Rosie's ears.

Matilda and her family lived in a teapot in a cottage. They were house mice. Today Matilda was travelling into the country to marry George, who was a field mouse. They had met on vacation. A sandcastle Matilda was making collapsed on top of her and George pulled her out. They became close friends.

Now, splendid in a beautiful lace wedding dress, Matilda stood with her family on the beach, watching the sky for George.

As he floated along, George could see them all waving below him. Matilda's veil was streaming out in the wind and the little ones were jumping up and down beside her.

George lowered the balloon by loosening the string and letting some air escape, and soon the basket dropped down onto the sand. Greetings were exchanged and George and Matilda hugged each other. Then George stowed away Matilda's suitcase. She had packed her trousseau in it – all the things she had made for her new home with George. There was a patchwork quilt, a shell-covered box for treasures, and her everyday apricot-colored dress, rolled up in her headscarf.

When they were ready to go, George, Oliver, and Humphrey blew up the balloon again. Then, with Matilda's veil blowing in the wind, they floated up and up, across the sand, as the mice cheered.

They drifted across a patchwork of fields and trees, until at last they arrived at Tree Stump House.

The huge table had been covered with delicious cakes and puddings and nuts. There were garlands of flowers everywhere.

The mice climbed out, and George put on his best gray coat and top hat. Then the wedding began. Everyone stood absolutely still, the bride and bridegroom in the middle and all the other mice in a circle around them. Finally, the oldest mouse stepped forward. He took George's paw and placed Matilda's paw carefully on top, and then he wrapped a daisy stem right around them, to show that the mice hoped to stay together forever. Then all the other mice stepped forward from the circle in turn, each carrying a little rush basket containing a small gift – acorns, biscuits, and some special herbs to use as medicine and for cooking.

After the ceremony, George and Matilda joined paws and all the others danced, weaving in and out of a daisy chain around them. When it was nearly dark the mice lit torches and George fetched his wedding present for Matilda from his secret workshop. It was a beautiful cart.

Matilda settled herself comfortably inside and all the mice sang a special farewell song as the newlyweds set off into the darkening woodland to begin their search for a home together.

They had decided to go into town to find a home. George liked to invent machines and he hoped to find useful things in people's garbage cans. Matilda loved exploring, and she was eager to see a town.

As evening came they found that the houses they passed were getting closer together and that the ground under their feet was becoming very hard. They were amazed by the size and noise of the cars and trucks on the road, and they stayed close to the walls of the shops and buildings they passed.

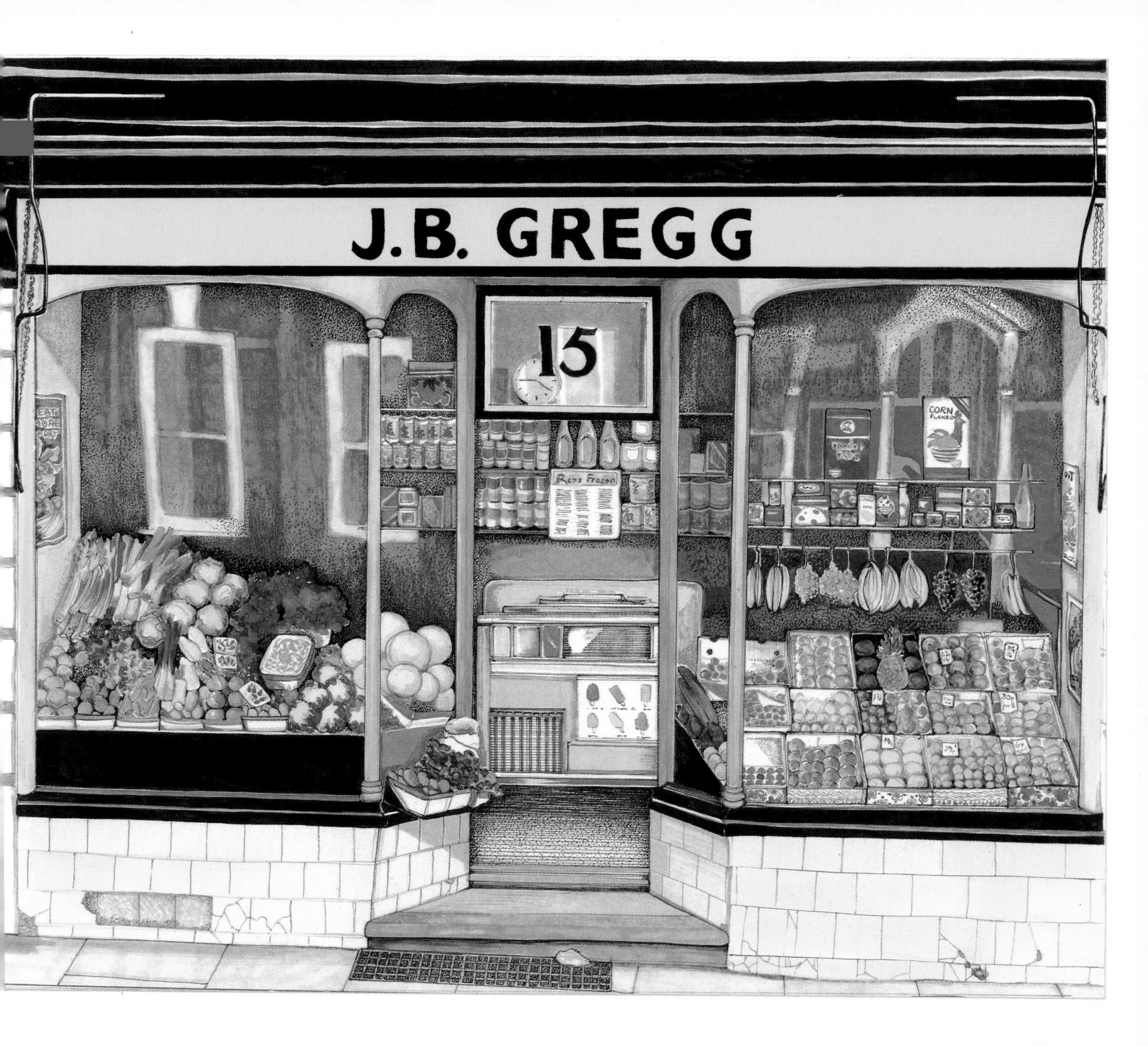

No one noticed the two small mice
as they stopped to gaze up at the
window of a grocery.
The colors of the fruit and vegetables
looked like patchwork to Matilda.

They came finally to a battered garden gate with a hole underneath it, and George, who felt very tired, decided to stop. He pulled the cart under the gate and looked around him.

Just beside their little cart was a large gray metal thing with a handle and spout. It was a watering can. George climbed up the side and peered in.

It looked warm and dry and would make a good place to spend the night, hidden from any cats. He quickly collected flowers, twigs and leaves and dropped them down inside. He made a nest, and fetched Matilda, who had fallen asleep wrapped in their quilt. She would have a lovely surprise, he thought, when she woke in the morning.

Matilda was indeed surprised when she woke. She was floating in a boat, with George snoring happily beside her. Above the watering can on the garage wall was a garden tap which must have been dripping all night. George and Matilda were now bobbing along in their nest, quite near to the spout opening in the can. Matilda woke George and they swam to the spout hole, pulling their patchwork quilt with them and using the lace train on her dress as a rope to tie themselves together with. They squeezed and squeezed up the spout and eventually popped out of the end like corks from a bottle. For a moment they lay shivering with fright in the grass below. Then quickly they collected Matilda's headscarf containing their everyday clothes and set off to search for a safer home.

GALLON

They had hardly had time to look around when they saw a moving shadow and realized as they caught her scent that there was a cat in the bushes. The two mice clung to each other.

Groping along the wall in the green darkness, they found a metal door covered in spider webs. Still worried about the cat, they carefully pushed their way into what looked like an old dolls' house. There was a kitchen table, a china-covered dresser, and logs in the fireplace. George and Matilda looked at one another excitedly. They had found their new home.

Before they dared to climb the stairs they squeaked together, to see if anyone was there. But there was no answer.

They found lots of spider webs on the landing, a metal bathtub and a bedroom. There were logs ready in the fireplace, a dressing table with little drawers and, underneath it, a doll hat decorated with blue ribbon.

A ladder near the bath led to an attic where they found a cot, a rocking horse, and a wooden trunk full of tiny dolls and teddy bears. There was a Noah's Ark with all the animals lined up in pairs ready to go.

For the rest of the day the two mice cleaned and straightened things up. George got a fire going in the kitchen, and Matilda found a bucket to carry in water from a puddle outside.

After vigorous scrubbing and sweeping and lifting, the two mice began to feel very hungry, and then remembered that they had left all their food in the cart by the watering can. George said he would go back after dark to get it.

He scurried along the wall, twitching his whiskers carefully to sense any danger. He found the watering can easily because it was so large and gray, and there beside it was his little cart. But to his horror he saw it was on its side and a large black paw was patting it.

George froze. The moon slid out from behind the clouds and he saw the cat, sniffing the mouse smell on the cart. George stood dead still as he watched his cart being tapped and tossed into the air. It was sure to be ruined.

Then somewhere in the distance was the sound of a human voice calling and a metal plate banging against a stone step. The cat raised her head and ran to be fed. George sighed with relief.

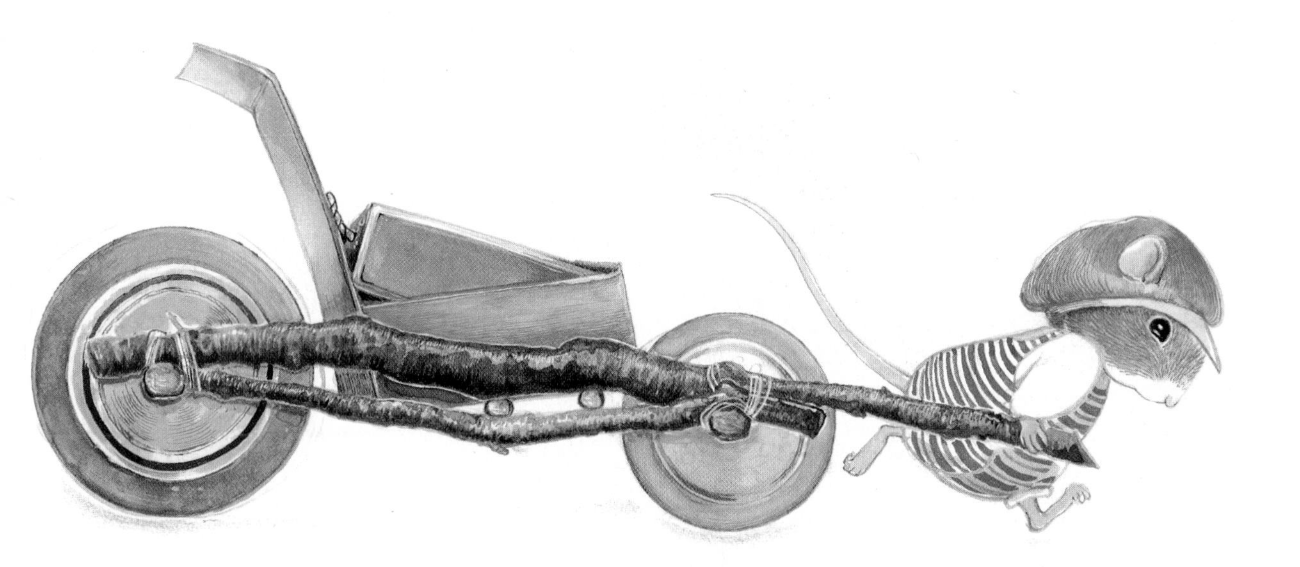

He ran as fast as he could and grabbed the cart, straightened it up, pushed the suitcase and their ptchwork quilt into it and ran and ran, pulling it roughly behind him till he reached the dollhouse.

George and Matilda were so glad to be safely back together again. They unpacked the remains of their wedding food and had a good supper in front of the fire. They they fell asleep, wrapped in their quilt.

CHOOSY
BEANS

The next day it was time for their first garbage can adventure. Both mice scurried through the ivy to the back of the house. The cat, locked up in the house, did not notice them. Moving quickly, they parked the cart by the garbage and George squeezed under the lid and slipped down inside.

It was *very* smelly – but wonderful. There were dozens of useful things. He threw down to Matilda a piece of soap, a plastic bag, apple peel, an assortment of cheese rinds, and a few baked beans. Matilda caught it all and packed it in the cart.

George slid down and brushed himself off. Then they scurred away unseen, as the cat lay fast asleep in the house, dreaming of a fish breakfast.

Back home, they continued to work on the dolls' house

They boiled water and used the soap, nibbled into smaller pieces, to wash all the curtains and bedclothes they could find. They heated up the old flat iron to press the curtains and then they sewed them carefully together where the material was frayed.

They polished the tile floor, which shone like a horse-chestnut. Then they polished the furniture with the inside of sliced acorns until the dressing table and chair were shining too.

By the time darkness fell, the linen was clean, and the two mice sat drinking hot acorn cocoa by a cozy fire in the bedroom. Then, feeling tired but happy, they curled up in a clean bed wearing doll nightgowns.

The next day they made a list of jobs to do.

George went around the house calling out what needed to be done. HOLE IN ROOF. RICKETY CHIMNEY. LEAVES IN HINGES. Matilda wrote it all down. Then she went outside and called out what she found in the garden. PARSLEY. HERB-ROBERT. SCURVY GRASS. MINT. PLANT CARROTS. MAKE WATER PUDDLE BIGGER. George wrote all this down and they set to work.

George had just started his climb to the roof by lassooing the chimney with rope when there was a tapping on the front door.

They were frightened. Could this be the real owner of the house? Matilda slowly opened the door. There on the step was an old gray mouse, leaning on a walking stick, holding a bunch of daisies.

"To welcome you," he said. When he looked past Matilda into the beautiful clean kitchen, he said, "Well, well, well."

Fergus Mouse did not own the dollhouse. He lived in an old boot hidden in the ivy nearby. He was very old and wise. He could remember the days when a little girl used to play with the dollhouse in the garden, and he could remember her going away with her parents a long time ago, and leaving the dollhouse behind.

He told George and Matilda everything he knew about the garden. There was a beautiful rock garden in the middle of the lawn under a lilac bush, with a stream that trickled over the rocks. Beneath the rocks and plants were hidden small doors to mouse homes and at night the eight mouse families living there crept out for parties and secret meetings. In the summer they splashed and swam in the pond.

In the spring the garden that Matilda had planted from discarded seeds yielded radishes and enormous carrots. George invented a special carrot harvesting machine and Fergus helped him operate it.

By September they had made lots of raspberry jam and stored it in glass jars. They filled the storage bin with twigs for cold days, and carrot wine was stored in the cellar for special occasions.

Sometimes a passing bird carried a letter back to Tree Stump House or the teapot cottage, and occasionally Matilda was able to send her mother a special piece of cheese for the children or a beautiful scrap of material she had found in the dustbin. Letters were delivered to the doll's house too, dropped like parachutes in the garden. It was good to have news of home.

Late in November Matilda and George had a wonderful piece of news to send. They thought that they would have babies of their own by Christmas.

Matilda had grown rounder and was often up in the attic choosing places for her babies to sleep, and imagining them playing with Noah's Ark.

On Christmas Eve, George brought in a fir tree branch decorated with berries and hung with acorn lanterns and he set it in the center of the kitchen.

Outside they could hear the rock garden mice singing carols across the garden and snow was beginning to fall softly.

It was nearly midnight, so George helped Matilda up the stairs, and once she was in bed he went on up to make sure that no snow was coming in through the patch on the roof.

When he returned to Matilda, there beside her on the pillow were five small pink mice, fast asleep. He touched each one very shyly. "What a lovely Christmas," he said, and put his paw gently round Matilda. Then he hung up seven doll socks at the foot of the bed, and all the mice slept.

As George made acorn tea in the morning, a passing robin dropped a parcel in the garden, so he hurried out into the snow to fetch it and put it under the Christmas tree.

The mouse family found lovely things in their stockings, a gold ring for Matilda, an oil stone for George to sharpen things with, and peanut rattles for the babies.

Then George trudged through the deep snow to Fergus's boot. He brought him back to share Christmas at the dolls' house and to see the babies.

When he arrived they all hugged each other and opened their parcels by the tree.

Fergus had a patchwork waistcoat, and he brought them a map of the garden, showing all the secret mouse houses. Matilda had a necklace George made by using colored beads he found in the dustbin. She had made George a notebook in which he now proudly wrote down the names they had chosen for their babies.

Last of all they opened the parcel which the robin had brought, and found a knitted shawl from Matilda's mother and a snowdrop carefully wrapped in cotton wool, from her father.

Then they all had stilton cheese and carrot wine to celebrate their first wonderful Christmas in the dolls' house.

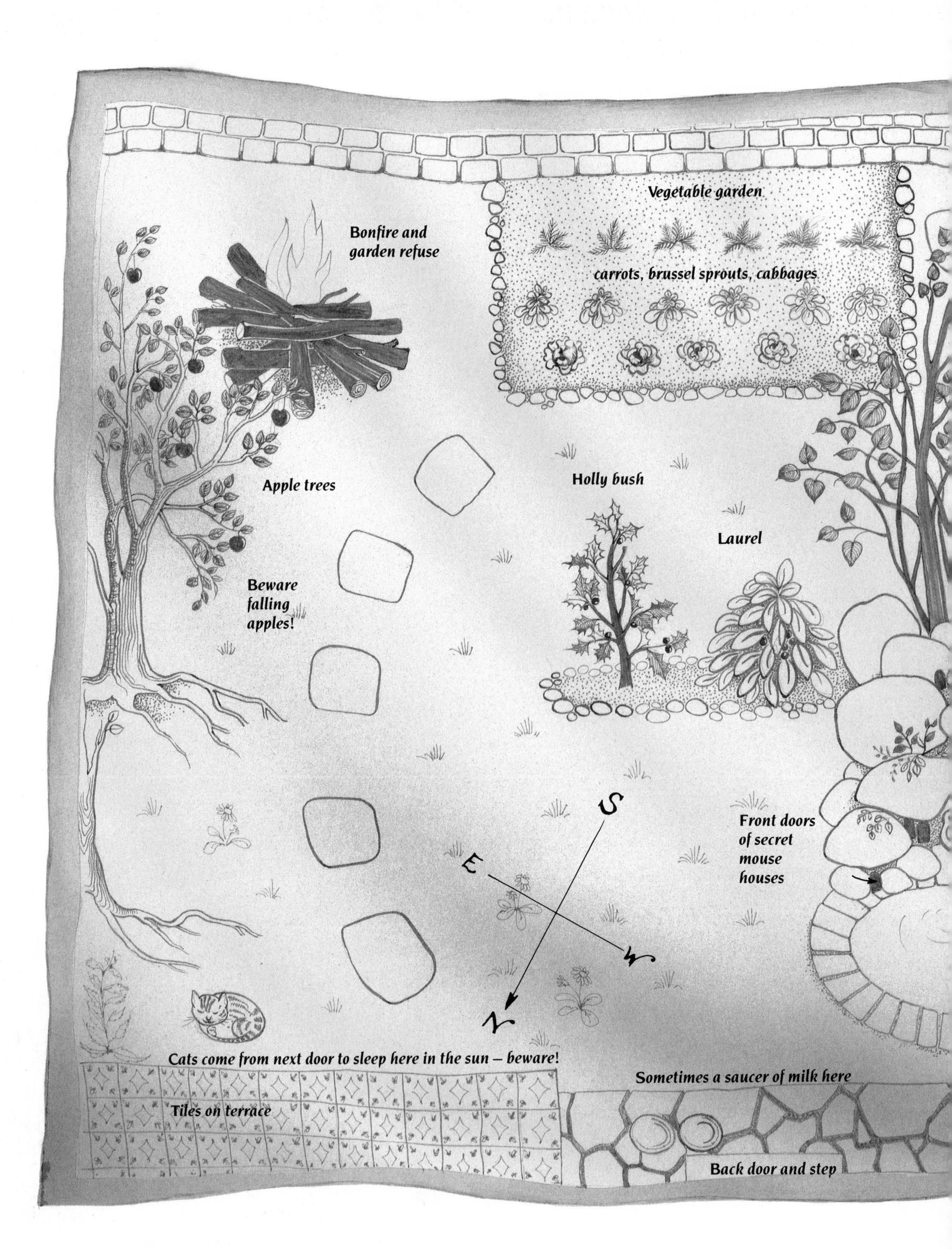
Vegetable garden
Bonfire and
garden refuse
carrots, brussel sprouts, cabbages
Apple trees
Holly bush
Laurel
Beware
falling
apples!
S
E
W
N
Front doors
of secret
mouse
houses
Cats come from next door to sleep here in the sun – beware!
Sometimes a saucer of milk here
Tiles on terrace
Back door and step